George

Melissa

Chaz

Melinda

Chico

CLARION BOOKS • 215 Park Avenue South, New York, New York 10003 • Text copyright © 2011 by Lindsay Lee Johnson • Illustrations copyright © 2011 by Carll Cneut • The text for this book was set in 20-point Artcraft. • The illustrations were executed in acrylic paint. • All rights reserved. • For information about permission to reproduce selections from this book, write to Permissions, Houghton Mifflin Harcourt Publishing Company, 215 Park Avenue South, New York, New York 10003. • Clarion Books is an imprint of Houghton Mifflin Harcourt Publishing Company. • www.clarionbooks.com • Library of Congress Cataloging-in-Publication Data • Johnson, Lindsay Lee. • Ten moonstruck piglets / by Lindsay Lee Johnson ; illustrated by Carll Cneut. • p. cm. • Summary: On the night of the full moon, ten piglets go out adventuring while their mother is fast asleep. • [1. Stories in rhyme. 2. Pigs—Fiction. 3. Animals—Infancy—Fiction.] I. Cneut, Carll, ill. II. Title. • PZ8.3.J6344Ten 2011 • [E]—dc22 • 2010005443 • Manufactured in China • LEO 10 9 8 7 6 5 4 3 2 1

For my husband, Neil, who invented the great Mama Piggy game, and for all the little piglets: Leisha and Jessie, Mikayela, London, Parker, Carter, Joshua, Samantha, Andrew, Madeline, and Sydney.
—L.L.J. (a.k.a. Meena)

4500265494

Ten Moonstruck Piglets

by Lindsay Lee Johnson

Illustrated by Caril Cneut

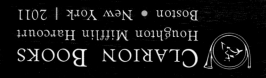

CLARION BOOKS

Houghton Mifflin Harcourt

Boston • New York | 2011

WHEN the full moon blooms bright
and fills up the night,
curious piglets
are dazed by the sight.

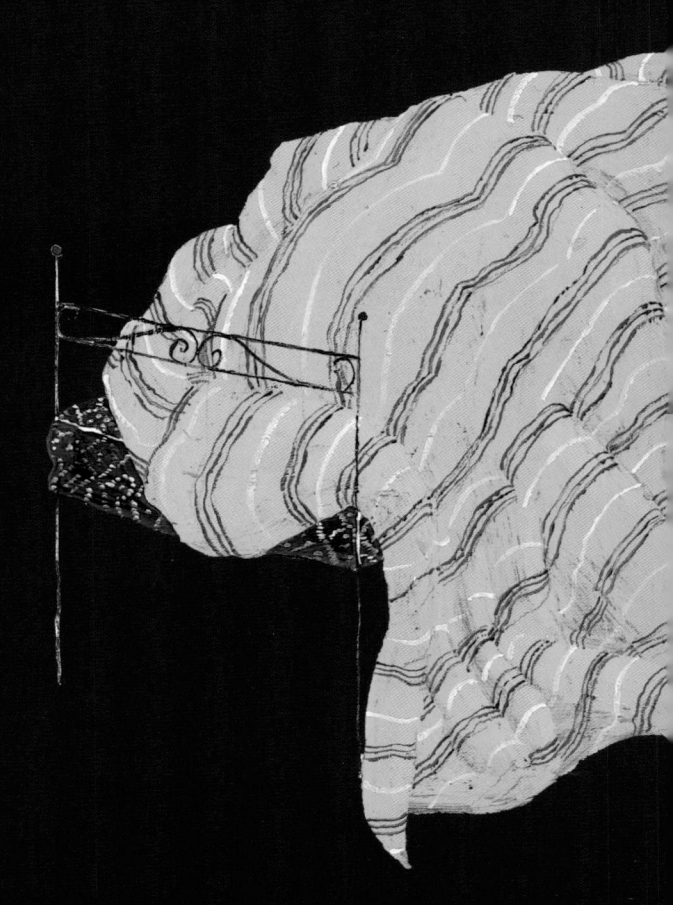

While Mama sleeps on,
to the light they are drawn.
Foolhardy piglets
skedaddle—they're gone!

All in a scramble,
all ready to gambol,
ten moonstruck piglets
on a midnight ramble.

Through the mud wallow,
beyond the wide hollow,
leapfrogging piglets
in turns lead and follow.

Under fences they scoot.
In gardens they root.
Snout-snuffling piglets
plunder and loot.

Over the creek they hop.
Into the pond they plop.
Belly-first piglets
recklessly flop.

In meadows they dance.
In fields they prance.
Wild, giddy piglets
in a moonlit trance.

They squeal! They snort!
On legs so short,
rollicking piglets
gaily cavort.

They frisk and whirl!
They caper and twirl!
Carefree pink piglets
with tails all a-curl.

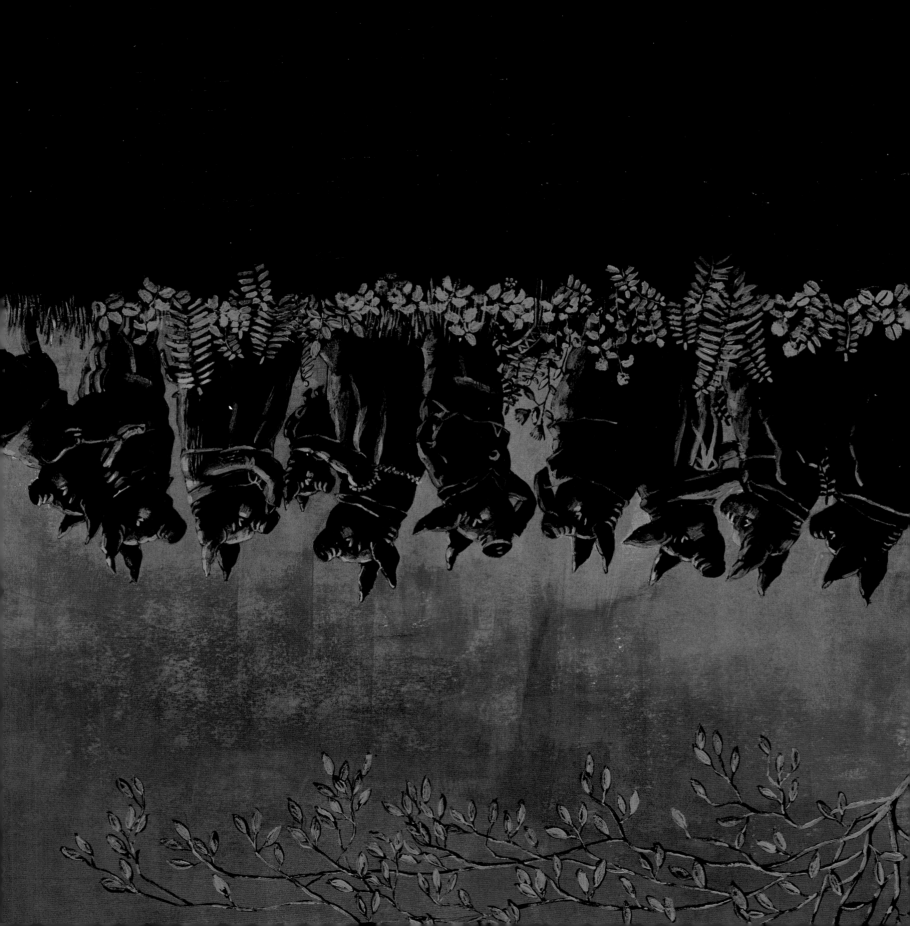

Soon clouds hide the moon
and deep shadows loom.
Runaway piglets
are lost in the gloom.

Then "Hoot!" cries an owl,
and fox comes to prowl.
Jowl-twitching piglets
scatter and howl. "MAMA!"

She wakes with a grunt,
quickly takes to the hunt,
calling her piglets,
tracking each runt.

She stomps through the clover,
finds every last rover,
sheepish wee piglets
whose night romp is over.

Back home in a heap
where the straw is so deep,
droopy-eyed piglets
tunnel swiftly to sleep.

Too soon the sun glows.
Too soon the cock crows.
Still moon-weary piglets
roll over and doze.

Bam

Lucy

Mia

Kelly

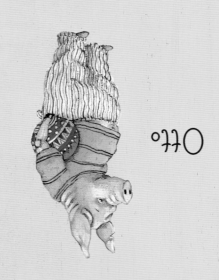

Otto